P9-BYS-203

by Sylvia Rouss
Illustrated by Holly Hannon

PITSPOPANY
NEW YORK ◆ JERUSALEM

Published by Pitspopany Press

Cover Design: Benjie Herskowitz

ISBN: 1-930143-17-6

Pitspopany Press titles may be purchased for fundraising programs by schools and organizations by contacting:

Marketing Director, Pitspopany Press
40 East 78th Street, Suite 16D
New York, New York 10021
Tel: (800) 232-2931
Fax: (212) 472-6253
Email: pop@netvision.net.il
www.pitspopany.com

Printed in Israel

The pictures in this book are dedicated
to my husband, Wes Hamilton,
with love

H.H.

ALSO IN THIS SERIES:

The Littlest Frog
The Littlest Candles

Noah!

"I want you to build a special boat, called an Ark," God told Noah.

"I will bring you two of every animal..."

As Noah stood at the entrance of the Ark, he looked up at the long line of animals forming in front of him.

Just as God had told him, there were two of every animal and bird, even of the little creeping creatures.

"Stay in line," Noah told the animals. "There will be room for all of you."

From THE JEWISH CHILDREN'S BIBLE
Adapted by Sheryl Prenzlau (Pitspopany Press)

The animals watched wide-eyed, in awe,
As Noah worked hard with hammer and saw.

They watched him all day, and as it grew dark,
The parrot exclaimed, "I believe it's an Ark!"

Early next morning, as bees began humming,
Wise Noah announced, "Soon rain will be coming!

"There'll be a great flood. It will cover the land.
I'm afraid you won't find a dry place to stand.

"God has asked me to build this huge wooden boat,
Which will save us all, and keep us afloat."

Noah told the animals to line up, two of each kind.
"Let's make sure that we leave no two behind."

As the animals gathered two by two,
The littlest pair came into view.

"The termites are coming!" cried a large kangaroo.
"Somebody dooo something!" begged the cow with a moo.

The giraffe shook his head 'til his neck felt quite sore.
The lion began pacing and started to roar.

The spider stopped spinning the web she was making.
Her heart was aflutter. Her legs began shaking.

When the two little termites got into their places,
All around them they saw angry animal faces.

"Hello everybody," they whispered a greeting,
And all of a sudden the sheep began bleating.

"You'll eat all the baaark and the lumber too.
When the Ark begins sinking, what will we do?"

The hyena stopped laughing and let out a howl.
"Whooo invited you two?" screeched a frightened old owl.

The rhinoceros bellowed, “You two are pests!
Don’t you realize you’re unwanted guests.”

“You must be crazy!” squawked a furious loon.
“Will the Ark be your dinner?” screamed the baboon.

Seeing the animals get madder and madder,
Made the littlest pair feel sadder and sadder.

Noah ignored the animals' protests and cries,
And welcomed the termites who had tears in their eyes.

"We know you are frightened. We know what you think,
But we would never make Noah's Ark sink."

When the last creatures boarded, rain began dripping.
The deck became slick. They all began slipping.

The elephant almost fell off of the Ark,
And right up his trunk slid a startled aardvark.

"Whoa!" said the horse as he started to stumble,
And just at that moment the goats took a tumble.

"What can we do?" Noah asked with a shout.
"We have to stop all this sliding about."

"Perhaps we can help," said the littlest pair.
Now everyone's eyes looked down with a stare.

"We can make sawdust to give you some traction.
Just say the word and we'll spring into action."

Some leftover wood, Noah gave to the two.
He anxiously watched as they started to chew.

Soon there was sawdust in everyone's stall.
The Ark might sway, but no one would fall.

"We're sorry," they said to the littlest pair.
"We weren't too nice. We were very unfair."

Now Noah spoke to the animals, large and small.
He looked at each one. He looked at them all.

"The way you treated the termites was terribly wrong,
But I'm glad you've decided we can all get along.

"It's important to accept each other's ways,
Cause we'll be together for at least forty days!

"So let's put an end to anymore hurtful chatter,
We're all God's creatures and to God, we all matter."

Mr. & Mrs. Termite
MR. & Mrs. PRAYING MANTIS

The termites just smiled, looking happy...and fatter.